a lesson
my cat taught me

To DAVID
EVERY BOOK
IS A
NEW
ADVENTURE

BEST WISHES
Saul Weber

by Saul Weber

SAWEB Books, Inc – New York

Second Edition

Interior and Cover Illustrations
Nancy Lepri

SAWEB Books Inc.

PUBLISHED BY SAWEB BOOKS, INC.

Printed in the United States of America
Copyright © 2007 Saul Weber
All rights reserved.

ISBN: 1452810885
ISBN 13: 9781452810881

Dedication

To all cat lovers and people who can
accept others for who they are
and not what they are.

Acknowledgments

My wife Hillary who suggested
I write a children's book.

My two cats whose antics were the
inspiration for my book.

Maura D, Shaw who was the first
person to tell me what I had written
for my book was publishable.

Jennifer lived in an apartment building with her parents and her Maine Coon cat, Mr. Tickles. He used to live at the local animal shelter before Jennifer and her parents adopted him.

The people at the shelter showed Jennifer a large cat named Mr. Tickles. When Jennifer wiggled her fingers near his cage, he licked them, and she liked that.

When they took him out of his cage so she could have a closer look, Jennifer liked the way he purred and smiled at her as she scratched and tickled him under his chin. *Now I know why he's called Mr. Tickles, she thought.*

Mr. Tickles turned out to be an extremely friendly cat. Whenever Jennifer would let him out into the hallway on her floor, he jumped at every opportunity to run up to strangers. Rubbing his head against their legs, he hoped they would reach down to pet him, and scratch him under his chin.

While he was in the hallway, Mr. Tickles also liked to sneak into other apartments. One day when Jennifer's neighbor, who also had a cat, left his door open; Mr. Tickles ran inside the apartment. Once there he made himself right at home by eating some of the neighbor's cat food; forgetting that he'd already eaten at his own home.

Mr. Tickles loved Jennifer. He sat on her lap as she watched TV in a chair, or lay down next to her if she was on the floor. When she went to sleep, he would sleep next to her feet.

Jennifer felt sorry about leaving him home alone while she was at school. Many times, Jennifer hoped to some day find another cat to adopt. Then, Mr. Tickles could have someone to play with while she was gone.

~

One day, Jennifer went with her mother to get their car. In the garage, Jennifer saw a skinny calico cat. When it came over and rubbed its head against her leg. Jennifer turned to her mother and asked, "Mom, may we take this cat home with us so Mr. Tickles can have a friend while I'm at school?"

"Not now dear. We have to go shopping at the mall for your new school clothes. Besides, we don't have Mr. Tickles' pet carrier with us, so we can't bring the cat home now."

~

After they came back from the mall, Jennifer asked, "May we get the cat we saw in the garage now? May we? Please?"

"In a few minutes dear, I want to put your new clothes in your closet first."

Once her new clothes were put away, Jennifer's mother picked up Mr. Tickles' pet carrier and called out, "Okay, Jennifer! Let's go down to the garage and see if we can find that cat."

"Do you think it will be waiting for us?" Jennifer asked.

"It's hard to tell, stray cats roam all over the neighborhood. You never know where they'll turn up next."

"I hope it will be there, Mom."

"I hope so too," said Jennifer's mother.

As soon as they waked into the garage, the calico cat came running up to them. It went straight to Jennifer and rubbed its head against her leg.

"That's good Jennifer! Hold the pet carrier while I try to get the cat into it."

The moment Jennifer put the carrier down, the cat walked right into it, almost as if it knew it would be getting a new home; a home that would be clean, dry and warm, and where it would find plenty of food and water.

As they walked back to their apartment, Jennifer heard the cat's loud purring. "Mom, I think the cat is happy to be coming home with us."

"I think you're right, Jennifer."

When they reached the door to their apartment, Jennifer asked, "Do you think that Mr. Tickles will like our new cat?"

"That's hard to say. Sometimes cats don't like having a strange cat come into their home, and sometimes they may start fighting."

"That's not nice, Mom! All animals should learn to live together."

When they opened the apartment door, they saw Mr. Tickles sitting near the door waiting for them. As he sat on the floor and watched as Jennifer's mother placed his carrier on the floor and then opened its door.

Out walked the new cat. It glanced at Mr. Tickles, and then turned left and began to explore its new home. *Poor Mr. Tickles,* Jennifer thought, *the new cat ignored him.*

Mr. Tickles sat there, staring at the new cat as it walked around the apartment. After the new cat was finished exploring the apartment, he started to walk over to it.

Sounding worried Jennifer asked, "Mom, because our new cat is in Mr. Tickles' home, do you think they will fight?"

"I don't think so. His fur isn't puffed up and he's walking slowly. Let's be ready to break them apart in case they do fight."

As they watched Mr. Tickles walk over to the new cat. It lowered its body and head, knowing the area belonged to Mr. Tickles.

When Mr. Tickles reached his new roommate, he began to smell it. He sniffed it from its head all the way down to its tail. When he finished, Mr. Tickles licked the new cat's head.

"Mom, I think Mr. Tickles likes his new friend – he's licking it all over its head," exclaimed Jennifer.

"You're right dear, he does seem to like her; otherwise he wouldn't be doing that."

"How do you know that the new cat is a girl?"

"She is a calico; and almost all calicos are girls."

"Does that make her special? Are there any boy calicos?"

"There are some boy calicos, but not many. I don't know why calicos are usually girls, dear. I only know that they are. So it does make her special."

"So may we keep her? Please?" Jennifer pleaded.

"Yes, but if they start fighting, we'll have to take her to the animal shelter where we found Mr. Tickles."

"Don't worry, Mom. I think they like each other."

As they watched, Mr. Tickles continued to lick his new friend's head, Jennifer asked, "Do you think she's hungry? Should we feed her?"

"Yes, however, I think it's a good idea if she has her own food and water dish."

"May I get them out for you?"

"Yes, they're on the bottom shelf where we keep the cat food."

Jennifer found the bowls in the cabinet and gave them to her mother.

"We'll need to wash these dishes before we use them; they're a little dusty," Jennifer's mother said.

"Why do we have to use different dishes? I thought they could share their food."

"That's a nice idea Jennifer, but we don't want them to start fighting over food. Mr. Tickles might not like sharing his food; especially they're both trying to eat at the same time."

Jennifer's mother placed the fresh food and water in the clean dishes. "Why don't you call Mr. Tickles to come and get his food?"

"Okay. Do you think the new cat will come too, when I tap on the empty cat food can?"

"Let's just see what happens when you do."

As soon as Jennifer's spoon hit the empty cat food can, their new cat came running. She stopped and looked at Jennifer and her mother.

"Look Mom, our new cat is already here!" exclaimed Jennifer, "She's looking at us as if she knows we're going to feed her."

"I had a feeling something like this might happen."

"Why?" asked Jennifer.

"This cat acted very friendly from the moment we first saw her. And sometimes people 'throw away' their pets because their pets they aren't wanted anymore."

"That's not nice," Jennifer frowned.

As Jennifer watched the calico, Mr. Tickles leisurely walked over for his food. He stopped and looked up at Jennifer and her mother.

"Meow! Meow!" yowled Mr. Tickles. He seemed to say, "Put the food down already, so I can eat."

After placing the food in front of their cats, Jennifer noticed how fast her new cat was eating. "Mom, our new cat has eaten up almost all of her food," exclaimed Jennifer.

"I noticed. She must have been starving."

"I hope she won't get sick for eating her food so fast," said Jennifer. She remembered that happened to her last month."

"Don't worry Jennifer; cats know how much food they need, and how to eat it."

"Our new cat is cleaning herself now, just like Mr. Tickles does. I wonder where she learned how to do that?"

"Cats have a natural instinct to keep themselves clean," replied Jennifer's mother.

"Mom… I think it's time to show her where the bathroom is."

"Oh, I knew I forgot something."

"What did you forget?" asked Jennifer.

"I forgot to find something to use as a litter box."

"Can she use the same one as Mr. Tickles?"

"Cats usually like to have their own place. Hmm, let me get that dishpan I was planning to throw out."

Jennifer's mother got the dishpan, and after filling it with some fresh litter, she placed it in the second bathroom. Mr. Tickles' box was in the other bathroom. "Jennifer, you can bring her into the bathroom now."

Jennifer brought her new cat to the litter box, and as soon as she saw the box, she started to use it.

After she finished, Jennifer picked it up her new cat. When she scratched and petted her calico -- like she did with Mr. Tickles -- the new cat began purring -- just like Mr. Tickles.

Jennifer finally had a chance to examine her new cat's face. When she did, she noticed that her new cat only had one eye. "Mom, our new cat has only one eye!" cried Jennifer.

"Don't cry honey…maybe that's the reason no one wanted her."

"Why would someone throw her away? That's a terrible thing to do! Why didn't they take her to a shelter, so she could find a new home?"

"I can't answer your question, but now it doesn't matter. She definitely has a new home with us," her mother exclaimed.

"Do you think she'll have a problem getting around the apartment?"

"She'll be fine. After she learns where everything is, she'll be very comfortable in her new home."

"Do we have to do anything special so it's easier for her to do things?"

"Animals do very well overcoming their disabilities. Do you remember last month, on *Animal Planet,* we saw a three-legged dog running around, jumping on and off things?"

"Yes," said Jennifer excitedly. She had a big smile on her face and her tears were gone.

"Well, the dog learned how to adapt on its own. There wasn't anyone around to teach him how to run and jump with three legs."

"I think Uno will be just fine here," smiled Jennifer

"Uno?" asked Jennifer's mother.

"That's her new name."

"How did you pick out that name?"

"Well, last week our teacher began to teach us another language. She said it's important for us to able to talk to someone that can't speak English."

"So, why did you choose Uno for her name?"

"The first thing we learned is how to count to twenty in Spanish. Uno is the number *one* in Spanish, and our cat only has *one* eye. So, her name is Uno."

"That's a great name for her, Jennifer, it also sounds nice. I think she'll like it."

"How do I teach her, her new name? Mr. Tickles already knew his name…."

"Scratch and pet her while saying her name. Also, call Uno when it's time to feed her. She will quickly learn her name."

Jennifer did as her mother suggested.

~

About three weeks later, Jennifer woke up from a nap to find Uno gone. Jennifer called out, "Uno. Uno." A moment later, Uno came and jumped up onto the bed.

"Hi Uno," said Jennifer while scratching the top of Uno's head;, "looks like you know your name already."

Happily, Jennifer ran to her mother, with Uno following close behind. "Mom, Mom! Uno knows her name!"

"That's wonderful," Jennifer's mom exclaimed.

"Do we have anything special I can give her? Like a treat?"

"I'm sorry; there isn't anything in the house right now. I'll buy something when I visit the pet shop later. They need more cat food, too."

"Great! As soon as I get the treats, I can start teaching her some tricks."

"That's okay for Uno, Jennifer, but you can't forget about Mr. Tickles."

"Okay, I'll teach him the same tricks as well."

Later that afternoon, Jennifer anxiously waited for her mother to return from the pet shop.

"Now remember, these are just for a treat. I think we should set a limit of two or three for each cat," said Jennifer's mother.

"Okay Mom, and thank you for getting the treats for me to use."

"You're welcome Jennifer."

Jennifer went to her room, sat down at her desk, and called out, "Mr. Tickles. Uno." Immediately both cats came running and sat in front of her. She shook the can of treats and then opened it. Taking a treat out, she held a piece in front of Mr. Tickles' nose. After he smelled it, Jennifer raised the treat about a foot over his head–he just stared at it.

Again and again, Jennifer held the treat just out of reach. Mr. Tickles watched it, but wouldn't reach with his paws for it.

Even though Jennifer was disappointed, she didn't want to tease Mr. Tickles, so she gave him the treat anyway. She placed the treat on the floor and watched as he ate it.

Meanwhile, Uno sat close by and watched the "action."

Jennifer was surprised when she tried the same trick with Uno. Reaching with her paws, Uno guided the treat into her mouth. *Wow, what a difference,* Jennifer thought.

Eagerly, she repeated the trick, but held the treat higher. This time, Uno sat down when she couldn't reach the treat.

After staring at the treat for a minute, Uno stood up on her hind legs, reached with her paw, and begged for the treat. Jennifer lowered the treat until Uno could eat it from her hand. Looking at Jennifer, Uno waited for another treat.

"Sorry Uno. I know you must like them, but you may only two treats today. I have to save the rest for another day," said Jennifer, putting the closed treat container in her desk drawer

Jennifer was very happy, and ran to tell her mother what happened.

"Wonderful," exclaimed Jennifer's mother.

"I know... but I'm worried Mr. Tickles might be stupid...."

"Dear, when you're not interested in doing some things, you won't do them, even if you usually love to. Like you, sometimes cats and dogs, won't do a trick if they're not interested in it."

"I think I know what you mean Mom. Animals are like people, except they have four legs."

"That's right Jennifer. I'm very proud of you for understanding, many other people can't."

~

As the weeks went by Jennifer worked hard trying to teach her cats a new trick every few days. However, Mr. Tickles never seemed to be interested in doing any tricks, but he seemed to love watching Uno do them.

Once Jennifer was finished working with Uno on her tricks, Mr. Tickles would always go over to Uno and lick her head. Almost like he was telling her he was proud of her for learning all these new things.

Jennifer taught Uno to pick the hand that had the treat. She would hold a treat in one hand,

and then stick out both hands in front of her, fingers curled into fists. She would then stick out her pinky finger on the fist that had the treat. Uno quickly caught onto that trick.

In the next trick, Jennifer held out both fists, with a finger sticking out on each hand. She then wiggled her little finger on the hand with the treat. Watching Jennifer's hands, Uno looked puzzled.

Jennifer watched and waited while Uno tried to solve the puzzle. Uno finally reached for the fist with the moving finger.

Jennifer couldn't believe that her cat could learn the trick so fast, so she tried it again. When Uno looked at the two fists the second time, she knew immediately which fist held the treat.

After this, Jennifer thought about how many more tricks she could teach Uno to do.

"Jennifer! Come and get your supper; it's on the table."

"I'll be there in a minute, Mom."

When Jennifer sat down at the table her mother asked, "How is your training program coming along with Mr. Tickles and Uno?"

"I have to give Mr. Tickles an 'F'. He's not showing any interest in what I'm trying to teach him. He just seems to like to watch Uno learn her tricks."

"I'm sorry you're not having any luck with Mr. Tickles," replied her mother. "So how is Uno doing with her training?"

"If Uno was a person, she would be a straight 'A' student, like me. As soon as I finish teaching her one trick, she seems to want to learn to do another."

"That must make you feel very happy."

"It makes me feel very happy," said Jennifer, "and proud too!"

After eating her supper, Jennifer went back to her room to study and to get ready for school tomorrow.

The next day in school, Jennifer's class got a new student–Hillary, who had just moved into their town.

When Hillary, sitting in a motorized wheelchair, rolled into the classroom, the teacher said, "We have a new student today. Her name is Hillary.

Everyone in the classroom, except for Jennifer and her teacher, gasped and stared at Hillary—some were curious stares and others were not so nice. Jennifer thought, *Poor Hillary, she knows why they are staring at her.*

The teacher told Gloria, who sat next to Jennifer near the front door, "Please move to a desk farther back in the room. Hillary needs to be in the front row because of her wheelchair."

When the bell rang, Jennifer's classmates ran off to the lunchroom. Jennifer waited and walked with Hillary to show her the way there.

After arriving there, Hillary sat at one of the empty tables. Jennifer sat down across from her and thought, *I don't want Hillary to eat alone, especially on her first day here.*

"Jennifer, why aren't you having lunch with your friends?" asked Hillary. "I'm used to eating alone. I'm also used to being treated as if there was something wrong with me."

"I don't think there's anything wrong with you," said Jennifer.

Surprised, Hillary said, "Are you saying that because you feel sorry for me? Well don't–I can do many things for myself."

"I'm telling you the truth. I don't think there's anything wrong with you," Jennifer answered.

Hillary stared at her, still not quite believing Jennifer actually felt that way.

Jennifer told Hillary why she felt nothing was wrong with her. It was because of the lesson her new cat, Uno, taught her. The more Jennifer told the story of Uno, the more Hillary listened. She listened carefully to each word Jennifer was saying.

At the story's end, Jennifer said, "The lesson I learned from Uno is: Even though some people might appear to be disabled, sometimes they can do more than someone who is not disabled."

As they continued to talk, Jennifer and Hillary discovered they were neighbors. Hillary's family lived one below Jennifer in the apartment building they lived in. Jennifer invited Hillary up to her apartment that weekend to see Uno and watch her do some tricks.

When the bell rang Hillary turned to Jennifer, "Thanks for eating lunch with me, and helping me feel welcomed here." Together, smiling, they started back to their classroom.

On the way back, a group of their classmates passed Jennifer and Hillary. Someone yelled out, "Watch out Jennifer! Don't stay too close to her much longer, you might catch she has," as everyone else laughed in a cruel way.

"What was that about?" asked Jennifer.

"Oh, I always hear mean comments when I start at a new school and then try to make new friends," answered Hillary.

"That's not nice, and I'm going to tell them that."

"It won't work. They'll do it more and make fun of you too, because they think their teasing bothers us."

"Fine then, I am going to tell our teacher, Ms. Baker. She'll make them stop!"

"Please don't do that Jennifer. It will only make things worse," Hillary pleaded. "As a favor to me, please don't tell Ms. Baker."

"Okay Hillary, if you say so. But I'm only trying to be your friend."

"Thanks for being the best new friend I ever had Jennifer!" Hillary smiled as the two entered their classroom.

~

On Saturday, Hillary went to Jennifer's apartment, to see the tricks Uno could do. Amazed at what Uno did, Hillary said, "I now can see why you feel about disabilities the way you do."

Jennifer replied, "I was only doing what I felt was the right thing to do."

Jennifer and Hillary enjoyed each other's company until Hillary had to go home for supper.

"I see you have a new friend. She feels seems to be very nice," Jennifer's mother said after Hillary left.

"Thanks Mom, she is. I've got to go to my room now. The school's having a writing contest and I have to enter it by next Monday."

"Did they say what to have to write about?"

"Yes, it has to be about learning a lesson."

"Don't you want to eat? Remember, we're having your favorite for supper–spaghetti with meatballs, covered with lots of Marinara sauce and melted mozzarella cheese."

"I remember now! I was excited about Hillary liking me and Uno, and thinking about the contest; I guess I forgot."

After supper, Jennifer went to her room and began writing her short story. She finished her story on the following Sunday, the day before the deadline. On Monday, Jennifer handed in her story at the principal's office before going to her classroom.

Two weeks later, at the school's weekly assembly program, the principal announced the contest winner. Jennifer was amazed when she heard the principal call out her name.

She ran to the front of the auditorium where the principal gave her a beautiful certificate with a blue ribbon on it while everyone clapped.

When the principal asked Jennifer to say a few words, all she could say was "Thank you," before she walked back to her seat. As she walked back, everyone there clapped and waved at her. Jennifer smiled back, waving the certificate the principal just gave her.

Jennifer could not wait to get home and tell her mother the good news.

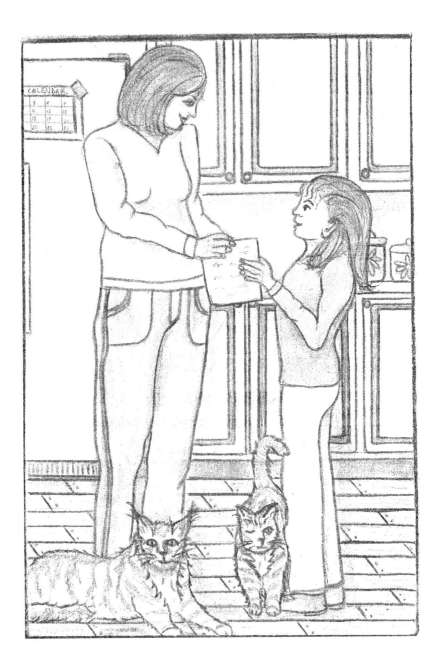

As soon as she got home, Jennifer ran to her mother and said excitedly, "Mom, Mom, Mom! I won the writing contest at school! The principal called my name during assembly and gave me this certificate. He also said it was a beautiful story." Jennifer held up her certificate for her mother to see.

"Congratulations, that's wonderful!" Jennifer's mother gave her a hug and a kiss. "What did you name your story?"

"I've got to thank Uno for that," said Jennifer. "It's called ***A Lesson My Cat Taught Me.***"